Clifford
and the
Big Parade

For Michelle Elizabeth Gere

The author thanks Manny Campana and Grace Maccarone
for their contributions to this book.

Copyright © 1998, 2011 by Norman Bridwell

ISBN 978-0-545-22323-2

10 9 8 7 6 5 4 3   11 12 13 14/0

Printed in the U.S.A.   40
First Scholastic printing, March 1998
This edition printing, June 2011

Clifford
and the
Big Parade

Norman Bridwell

Cartwheel
B·O·O·K·S ®

SCHOLASTIC INC.
New York   Toronto   London   Auckland
Sydney   Mexico City   New Delhi   Hong Kong

Clifford's town is 100 years old.
There will be games and a parade.

People dress in clothes from 100 years ago. Emily Elizabeth and Clifford dress up, too.

The first game is a log-pull.

Two horses have a hard time.

Clifford helps them.

Clifford sees a bike race.
He is too big to ride a bike.

But he can be in the race anyway.

Some people toss horseshoes.

Clifford wants to do it, too.
Emily Elizabeth stops him.

In the next game, Clifford
keeps his eyes on the ball.

He does not see the net.

Clifford sees a pie-eating contest.
Who can eat the most pies?

Clifford can!

Clifford is a mess.
Some birds help him.

Clifford is happy to feed them.

The parade will start soon.
The Parade Princess will have
lots of flowers.

Oh, no! Bees like flowers!

Clifford tries to shoo them away.

Then he tries to blow them away.
It works!

"Thank you," says the mayor.
"Would you lead the parade?"

Everyone is ready.

A man runs to the front.
"Stop the parade!" he shouts.

"We need help at the bridge," he says.

Clifford runs fast.

Clifford sees the bridge has fallen.
He thinks fast.

The parade goes on.
But Clifford is not in it.

He is under it!

Everyone thanks Clifford.

It is a very special day.